Minka Makes Her Mark

Amabel Barlow

Published by New Generation Publishing in 2022

ISBN: 978-1-80369-342-2

www.newgeneration-publishing.com

New Generation Publishing

Meet Minka, an artistic monkey
who loves doing art.
How does she do it?
She listens to her heart.
Her art is art-tas-tic!
Would you like to see?
Then let's go to her gallery with a 1, 2, 3!

1

She can paint flowers.

2

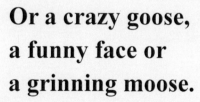

Or a crazy goose,
a funny face or
a grinning moose.

Her art can be...Odd?

Her art can be cool. She can paint anything. There is no rule.

Her art can be swirly...

Or in different shapes or lines
Whatever style she chooses…..
She hopes it all combines!

Her art can be quiet.

Her art can be LOUD!
Wherever she does it,
it makes her rather proud!

Minka can paint in any colour,
either purple, blue or red.

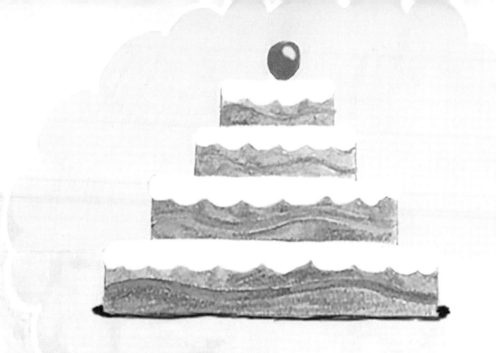

Where does she find great ideas?
She pictures them in her head.

Minka's art can be messy.
Her art can be clean.

She can paint whilst jumping on a trampoline.

13

She can paint with her paws, and paint with her toes.

Hey Minka look!
You have paint on your nose.

Minka loves her art.
It's such good fun to do.
With the power of a paintbrush,
You can be an artist too!

The End

Lightning Source UK Ltd.
Milton Keynes UK
UKRC031122150622
404465UK00001B/12